Fashion Disaster

Also by Jill Santopolo

Sparkle Spa

Book 9

Fashion Disaster

JILL SANTOPOLO

Aladdin

NEW YORK LONDON TORONTO SYDNEY NEW DELHI

ALADDIN

An imprint of Simon & Schuster Children's Publishing Division
1230 Avenue of the Americas, New York, NY 10020
This Aladdin paperback edition October 2016
Text copyright © 2016 by Simon & Schuster, Inc.
Cover illustrations copyright © 2016 by Cathi Mingus
Also available in an Aladdin hardcover edition.
All rights reserved, including the right of reproduction in whole or in part in any form.
ALADDIN is a trademark of Simon & Schuster, Inc., and related logo is
a registered trademark of Simon & Schuster, Inc.
For information about special discounts for bulk purchases, please contact
Simon & Schuster Special Sales at 1-866-506-1949 or business@simonandschuster.com.
The Simon & Schuster Speakers Bureau can bring authors to your live event. For more
information or to book an event, contact the Simon & Schuster Speakers Bureau
at 1-866-248-3049 or visit our website at www.simonspeakers.com.
Series design by Jeanine Henderson
Cover design by Laura Lyn DiSiena
The text of this book was set in Adobe Caslon.
Manufactured in the United States of America 0916 OFF
10 9 8 7 6 5 4 3 2 1
Library of Congress Control Number 2016936113
ISBN 978-1-4814-6392-8 (hc)
ISBN 978-1-4814-6391-1 (pbk)
ISBN 978-1-4814-6393-5 (eBook)

For my mom, who knows exactly what it means
to be strong and smart and sparkly

Glittery thanks to Karen Nagel, Miriam Altshuler,
Marianna Baer, Anne Heltzel, Marie Rutkoski,
and Eliot Schrefer

Contents

one

Purrfectly Purple

A ly and Brooke Tanner had gotten to the Sparkle Spa extra early on Sunday morning.

Their dog, Sparkly, was in his favorite corner of the spa, busy chewing on a piece of rawhide that was spiraled like a staircase.

Aly was busy finishing a blueberry muffin.

And Brooke was busy experimenting. She took out the elastic from the bottom of her braid, unbraided her hair, then took out the top elastic, letting her hair fall loose down her back.

"What do you think?" she asked Aly. Since Aly was in fifth grade and Brooke was only in third, Brooke often asked her older sister for advice. But sometimes, even though Brooke was younger, Aly asked *her* for advice. So it was pretty much even between them.

"Wow," Aly said. "I think your hair might have grown more overnight!"

Brooke's hair wasn't just long. It was *really* long. It was the kind of long where the bottom ends of it brushed the top of her shorts. She pulled some strands over her shoulders to the front side of her body.

"I think it goes past my belly button," Brooke said, lifting up her T-shirt to see where her hair stopped on her stomach. "Yep, definitely," she confirmed, pulling her shirt back down.

Aly inspected her sister. She braided Brooke's hair all the time, so Aly knew it was long, but because Brooke never, ever wore it down, Aly hadn't thought about just how long it had gotten. Brooke always had it in either one braid or two: sometimes a French braid, sometimes Dutch, sometimes a fishtail, or sometimes a regular braid. But it was always tied back somehow.

"I think you have mermaid hair," Aly told her sister.

Brooke's eyes lit up behind her blue-framed glasses. "You think so?" she said.

Aly nodded. "I do. But it's still kind of clumped into three pieces. Do you want me to brush it?"

"Do we have a brush here?" Brooke asked.

"I think there's one in the desk," Aly answered.

Brooke walked over to the other side of the Sparkle Spa—which was really just the back room of their mom's nail salon, True Colors—and found a brush the color of Purrfectly Purple nail polish in the desk drawer.

The girls had done their best to decorate the Sparkle Spa with colorful pillows and beautiful paintings and

a huge display of nail polish on multiple shelves—
in addition to the two teal pedicure chairs and two
blue manicure stations that were already there—but
some things had to stay, like their mom's desk and the
mini-fridge right next to it.

Brooke sat down on one of the pillows in the
nail-drying area, and Aly sat behind her, brushing
and brushing her sister's hair until it looked more
mermaidy than ever.

"When was the last time your hair was cut,
Brookester? At a real salon?" Aly asked. Aly had gotten a haircut about six weeks ago. She liked keeping
her hair chin-length like her mom's.

Brooke thought for a few moments. "Kindergarten?" she said. "Or maybe preschool?"

Aly quickly counted in her head. "Brooke!" she
said. "That's, like, three or four years ago!"

"Actually, I think I got a haircut right before

kindergarten started. I remember the pieces of hair made my new shirt itchy—the one with glitter hearts— and I was worried I wouldn't be able to wear it for the first day of school. But then Mom washed it, and it was fine. Remember that shirt? I wish it still fit."

"I remember," Aly said. "I had one just like it with glitter polka dots, and I wore it for the first day of second grade. So it's really been three and a half years since your hair was cut."

Brooke turned around to face Aly. "Want to know a secret?"

Aly nodded, but she was pretty sure her sister would have told her even if she hadn't.

"I've been thinking about getting a major hair-cut," Brooke said. "A super-short one, like yours and Mom's." Brooke took a bunch of her hair in her fist and looked at the ends.

"Really?" Aly asked. "But your hair's a little

different than mine and Mom's." Aly and her mom both had brown hair—Aly's straight and Mom's a tiny bit frizzier—while Brooke's was soft, blond, and wavy, like their dad's. Aly wasn't sure what Brooke's hair would look like if it were much shorter. It definitely wouldn't fall straight down like hers did.

Brooke shrugged. "I don't know. My other secret is that I'm a little scared to get a haircut. I mean, my hair has looked like this *forever.* Everyone kind of knows me as the girl who wears long braids. They might not know me anymore if I get a haircut."

Aly laughed, even though she tried not to. Her sister was a little bit nutty sometimes. "I think people will know you just fine with shorter hair. There's a lot more to you than your hair."

Brooke laughed now too. "I guess you're right," she said. "I have glasses and a big sister, and we run a nail salon, and I'm good at art."

"Exactly," Aly said. "And speaking of our nail salon, everyone should be here soon—our customers and Sophie."

"What about Charlotte and Lily?" Brooke asked.

"They're coming in late today," Aly told her. "Charlotte's cheering for Caleb at his basketball game, and Lily has her own basketball game."

Sophie, Charlotte, and Lily were Brooke and Aly's best friends and helped them run the Sparkle Spa.

Sophie was in third grade and was the third manicurist.

Charlotte and Lily were in fifth grade and in charge of different parts of the salon. Charlotte did all the organizing, so she had the title of COO (chief operating officer), whereas Lily took care of the money, so she had the title of CFO (chief financial officer).

And Brooke and Aly were co-CEOs (chief

executive officers)—that meant the sisters were in charge of everything.

Even though Aly kept asking Charlotte and Lily if they wanted to learn how to polish, neither of them did. They liked their current jobs just fine.

"Okay, let's set up, then!" Brooke said, hopping up from the ground. Her loose hair swished around and caught on a button on a pillow. She moved forward, but a piece of her hair didn't. "Ugh," she said. "But can you braid me first?"

Aly quickly braided her sister's hair—nothing fancy, just a low braid that didn't use an elastic on top. As she secured the bottom, she said, "You know, if you really do want to get a haircut, we can look through magazines to find people with your kind of hair and see what styles look best. I bet you'd look just as good with shorter hair as you do with long hair. We just have to find the right look."

Brooke smiled and tugged on her braid—something she did whenever she was excited or nervous. Something, Aly realized, she wouldn't be able to do if she cut her hair short. "Let's look later," Brooke said. "But that doesn't mean I'm cutting it for sure."

Aly nodded. "Of course not. Just doing some research."

And with that, Sophie poked her head into the Sparkle Spa and the girls got to work. All thoughts of haircuts zipped right out of Aly's mind. She wondered if the same thing was true of her sister.

two

Ever Green

A few hours later the Sparkle Spa was super busy. Once Charlotte arrived, she greeted all the customers, using her clipboard to check off the day's appointments and inform clients who would be doing their manicures or pedicures.

"Hi, Hannah," Charlotte said to a fourth grader who walked through the door. "You're with Sophie today. Please choose your color from the wall. We just got a new one called Ever Green that I think is really pretty."

"Does it go well with stripes?" Hannah asked. "Because I was thinking about stripes today."

Brooke turned her head from where she was polishing Clementine Stern's toes. "Perfect with stripes," she said. "Especially if you pair it with White Out or Silver Celebration. Those both look really good against Ever Green. I tested some out yesterday when the box of new colors was delivered."

Aly finished the final clear coat atop a Red Between the Lines manicure for Uma Prasad, a sixth grader Aly knew from school, and then led her to the drying area. On her way back to her station she stopped to ask Charlotte, "Who do I have next?"

Charlotte looked at the clipboard in front of her. "You've got Tuesday next," she said. "Then Daisy and then Parker—pedicures for the first two girls and a manicure for Parker."

Aly nodded just as Tuesday walked in the door.

"Hi, Tuesday," Charlotte greeted her. "You're with Aly today. Just pick your color and she'll get started."

Aly headed over to the second pedicure chair, to the left of the one Brooke was using. She loved how well the Sparkle Spa ran now and how many regular customers they had. Pretty much all of their clients returned once they'd had their nails done there the first time.

Just as Aly was helping Tuesday up onto the chair, she heard a voice yell, *"Stop everything!"*

Aly did stop. Brooke did too. And Sophie. But Charlotte did not. She kept blocking the doorway.

"Hey," she said, "you don't have an appointment."

"This is not *about* appointments!" the girl yelled, and then pushed passed Charlotte.

Aly heard Brooke groan.

It was Suzy Davis. Aly should have guessed. Ever since kindergarten, Suzy and Aly had been enemies, but just this year, things had gotten a little better. Then Suzy's uncle had married Joan, Aly and Brooke's favorite manicurist at True Colors, and Aly and Suzy had been junior bridesmaids together at the wedding. Because of that, they ended up kind of friendly. Not best friends or anything, but certainly not enemies anymore.

"Hey, Suzy," Aly said. "What's going on?"

Suzy thrust a doll out in front of her. The doll was wearing a dress the color of Cotton Candyland and had straight, dark, silky hair—kind of like Sophie's, except Sophie's was longer.

"Look," Suzy said. "Doesn't her hair look gorgeous?"

Aly shrugged. "Sure," she said. "But what's the big deal?"

Suzy cleared her throat. "I have figured out a way to make the Sparkle Spa the best spa in all the world."

Brooke stood up and put her hands on her hips. "It already *is* the best spa in all the world, Suzy Davis. We've had this conversation a million times already."

Sophie nodded in agreement.

Suzy just rolled her eyes.

But Aly was curious. Even if Suzy was a pain and didn't say things in the nicest way possible—or even in a way that was nice at all—she *did* have good ideas. "What's your idea this time?" Aly asked her.

"Haircuts!" Suzy said, thrusting the doll forward again. "I just cut this doll's hair, and it looks better than the haircut you got last month."

"Hey!" Aly said.

She waited for Brooke to say something, because Brooke *always* said something to Suzy Davis when she was mean, but Brooke was silent. Aly looked over, and her sister seemed deep in thought.

"So," Suzy continued, "I think that you should

turn part of the Sparkle Spa into a hair salon and that I should offer haircuts. Especially since your mom said I couldn't join the salon with my spectacular makeup services."

Twice, once at Auden Elementary's carnival and once on the school's Picture Day, Suzy had run her makeup business. Aly had mentioned inviting her to join the Sparkle Spa team as a makeup artist, but Mom had said no. Aly was pretty sure it was because Suzy had once stolen the list of all the Sparkle Spa's clients.

"The thing is," Charlotte said, "doll hair is different from human hair."

Aly nodded. "It's true, Suzy. Just because you can cut doll hair, that doesn't mean it would work the same way on a real person. Maybe you could open a doll hair salon?"

Suzy rolled her eyes again. "That's the lamest

thing I've ever heard. I'm not going to cut doll hair all day long." Then she scanned her eyes across everyone in the spa. "How about I prove I can cut people's hair? Who's going to let me give them a haircut?" she asked. "Clementine? Uma?"

"Sorry," Clementine said, "I just got a trim."

"Not me," Uma said. "I like my hair the way it is."

"You sure you don't want bangs?" Suzy asked. "I think they'd make your eyes look even bigger."

"Positive," Uma replied. "And my eyes look fine just the way they are, thank you very much."

"I'll do it," Brooke said.

Aly gasped. "What?" she said to her sister.

Brooke shrugged. "I was thinking about a haircut—you know we just talked about it—and the doll's hair does look great. Can you give me the same cut?" she asked Suzy.

"Of course," Suzy said.

Aly shook her head. "But, Brooke . . . that's *doll* hair. And it's *straight* doll hair. I don't think your hair will turn out the same."

Brooke looked at Suzy.

Suzy looked at the doll. "It'll look just like this," she said. "I even brought my own scissors."

Brooke nodded again. "Let's do it." Then she turned to Clementine and said, "I'll finish your toes in a minute."

"Are you sure you want to do this, Brooke?" Sophie asked quietly.

"Absotively posilutely," Brooke said. "I've been thinking about making a change, and then Suzy showed up offering one. It's like the whole universe wants me to get a haircut. This haircut was meant to be." That was what Mom said when things worked out perfectly. But Aly wasn't quite sure this was a meant-to-be moment.

Brooke got up and headed over to an empty

manicure station and sat down. "Is over here good?" she asked.

"Well," Suzy said, walking over to her, "for now. But not once I get my own space in a corner or something." She stood behind Brooke.

Aly felt like she should do more to stop this, but then again, maybe Suzy *was* right. Maybe doll hair and real-person hair were pretty similar. Maybe Brooke's haircut would look fantastic, like she was a movie star or something. And maybe the universe *did* want Brooke to get a haircut. Maybe it *was* meant to be. But Aly was definitely less certain about that than Brooke seemed to be.

"Okay," Suzy said, looking at Brooke's braid. "First, I'm going to cut off the braid. Then I'm going to do the styling part."

Brooke nodded, a smile on her face. "Do it!" she said.

Aly found herself shutting her eyes.

"Here I go!" Suzy said.

Aly heard the sharp sound of scissors slicing through hair.

Then she opened her eyes and gasped.

three
Pinktacular

W hat is it? Why did you make that sound?"
Brooke asked her sister.

Aly watched as Brooke's long braid slithered to
the floor like a snake. At almost the exact same time,
Brooke's hair fluffed up in the shape of a triangle
around her head. Aly gulped. "Just surprised is all,"
she said. "I haven't seen you with short hair since you
were a baby."

Then the salon went quiet as all the girls, in vari-
ous stages of manicures and pedicures, watched Suzy
continue to cut Brooke's hair.

Aly watched her snip along the bottom to make it even, but Brooke's hair didn't lie even. It was fluffy. And no matter what Suzy did, it stayed in the shape of a triangle. It did not look anything like the sleek bob on the doll Suzy had brought with her.

"Um," Tuesday said to Suzy, "do you have to wet it? That's what they do when I get my hair cut."

Suzy's face was starting to lose its usual confident look. "I didn't wet the doll's hair," she replied, "so I'm not going to wet Brooke's hair."

"But people hair and doll hair aren't the same," Charlotte repeated.

Brooke looked at the faces everyone in the Sparkle Spa was making. They weren't bad, but they weren't necessarily good, either. More like . . . concerned faces. "Can someone bring me a mirror?" she asked.

"No!" Suzy shouted. "I'm not done yet." She was walking slowly around the back of Brooke's head, like she was trying to figure out what to do next.

Suzy was holding Brooke's chin in one hand and the scissors in the other when Brooke and Aly's mom popped her head in from the main salon. "Hi, girls," she said cheerfully. And then she paused. "What is going on in here?" she asked, walking into the room.

No one answered. Aly had no idea what to say.

"Brooke," Mom said, very slowly, "what's happened to your hair?"

"How does it look, Mom?" Brooke asked. "Suzy's an expert doll haircutter and is giving me a haircut."

Mom pressed her lips together. Aly knew that meant she was upset. Very upset.

"No," Mom said, "Suzy is no longer giving you a haircut."

"But I'm not done yet," Suzy said.

"Yes," Mom answered, "you are. Please take your doll and your scissors and sit over there until I can call your parents." She pointed toward an empty pillow in the jewelry-making area.

"But—" Suzy started to object.

"Now," ordered Mom.

Suzy walked over and sat down.

"Can I see it?" Brooke asked. "Please?"

Mom went to her desk, pulled out a mirror, and brought it over to Brooke. The minute Brooke saw herself in the mirror, her eyes welled up with tears. *"Nooo!"* she wailed. "I want my hair back! This looks terrible. Suzy Davis, you made me look like that Sphinx statue we learned about in school when we were studying Egypt! My hair is a fluffy triangle!"

Mom took a deep breath. "Okay," she said. "Brooke, come with me. We'll get you an appointment at Snip to My Lou, and you won't look like the Sphinx anymore. Aly, you and Sophie take care of your customers for the rest of today. But later we're going to talk about how you let this happen. And, Suzy, I haven't forgotten about you. I'll call your parents after I make Brooke's appointment."

"I was just trying to give Brooke a good style," Suzy said.

"But you didn't!" Brooke cried.

Suzy looked down at the scissors in her lap. Aly could tell she felt bad. Suzy hadn't *meant* to make Brooke look like an old Egyptian statue.

Mom and Brooke walked out of the Sparkle Spa, but no one moved. Finally, Aly stood up. She was worried about Brooke's hair and about getting in trouble later, but she also had a business to run.

"Okay," she said. "Charlotte, can you rearrange the schedule so that Sophie and I take over Brooke's clients? And can you please call anyone whose time needs to be moved?"

"I can help polish," Suzy offered quietly.

Suzy was actually a very good polisher, but Aly had a feeling that was not the best idea at the moment. Mom seemed like she wanted Suzy out of the salon. "Thanks, Suzy," she said. "But we'll be okay—just me and Sophie. We've done it before, right, Soph?"

Sophie nodded. "We'll be fine."

"Who's going to finish my toes?" Clementine asked. "They're Pinktacular."

"I will," Aly said. "Let me just quickly clean up."

Aly headed over to where Brooke had been sitting and picked up her braid. It was weird to see it on the floor, not attached to Brooke's head. Aly walked toward the trash to throw it out, but she couldn't bring herself to do it. Instead, she dropped the braid in the bottom drawer of Mom's desk. She'd deal with that another time.

✳ ✳ ✳ ✳ ✳

A few minutes later Mom came into the salon and beckoned Suzy to come with her. After she left, the mood in the Sparkle Spa lifted. The girls who were waiting for their manicures and pedicures—or waiting for their manicures and pedicures to dry—started chatting again.

But even though things felt back to normal for everyone else, they didn't feel that way for Aly. Even more than wondering what kind of trouble she would be in, she was worried about Brooke and what in the world her haircut was going to look like after her appointment. Anything would be better than a blond, fluffy triangle that looked like the head of the Sphinx.

fouR

Souper Green

Joan drove Aly home that day. In addition to being the girls' favorite manicurist and Mom's best friend, she was the COO of True Colors—the person in charge of the salon when Mom wasn't around.

"So big happenings at the Sparkle Spa today," Joan said as they drove down Main Street, Sparkly sitting on Aly's lap.

"I should've tried to stop Brooke," Aly said with a sigh. "I did try a little, but . . ." Her voice trailed off.

Joan glanced over at Aly in the passenger seat, her hands firmly on the steering wheel. "I know your mom holds you responsible for everything in the Sparkle Spa, but this wasn't your fault, kiddo. Suzy wanted to cut hair, and Brooke volunteered, right?"

Aly nodded, stroking Sparkly's head. "Yes."

"Sometimes you can't save people from themselves," Joan continued. "If Brooke said Suzy could give her a haircut, then she has to take responsibility for that. The same way that if Mrs. Howard picks a really terrible color for her nails—"

"Like Souper Green?" Aly asked, naming a color that was almost an exact match for the pea soup served in her school's cafeteria.

"Like Souper Green," Joan agreed as she flicked the blinker signal on before making a right turn. "When Mrs. Howard picks Souper Green, all I can say is, 'Are you sure that's what you want?' If she says

'Yes,' I have to polish her nails that color, because she chose it. Even if I think it's a bad idea and would never want my own nails that color. So just because *you* wouldn't want Suzy to cut your hair, that doesn't mean you have to stop her from cutting everyone's hair on the planet."

Aly looked out the window and thought about that. "Not everyone's hair," she said to Joan. "Just Brooke's. Because Brooke is my sister and I *knew* it was a bad idea."

Joan shrugged. "Well, Brooke might have liked the haircut. You really had no way of knowing that."

Aly thought some more. It was an interesting point she hadn't considered. But at least a yucky nail polish color could be removed instantly. A person was stuck much, much longer with a yucky haircut.

Sparkly licked Aly's thumb. He'd been very quiet

during the ride home. For a moment Aly wondered if he was feeling okay, but then she returned to thinking about Brooke's haircut.

"I told your mom that, by the way," Joan said. "So I don't think you're going to be in any trouble when you get home."

"Thanks," Aly said. She wished she could hug Joan, but since Joan was driving and Aly had a dog in her lap, she figured it wasn't the safest idea. Joan really was the best, though. She fixed Aly's and Brooke's problems all the time. And she baked them delicious cookies too. Aly didn't know what she would do without Joan—or what Mom would do without her either.

Soon the car stopped in the Tanner driveway.

"This is you," Joan said when Aly didn't get out right away.

"I know," Aly replied. Then she unbuckled her

seat belt and gave Joan a big hug. "Thank you for the ride. And for talking to Mom, too."

"Anytime," Joan said.

"I'm home!" Aly yelled as she walked in the door. "Brooke? Mom?" She knew Dad had already left on a business trip earlier that day and wouldn't be back until Friday night, so she didn't bother calling for him.

"Upstairs!" Mom called back.

Aly put Sparkly down on the floor and headed toward the staircase. Sparkly didn't follow, he just curled up under the kitchen table. When Aly reached her and Brooke's room, she heard sniffling.

"Brooke?" Aly asked as she walked in.

Brooke quickly stuck her head under a blanket. "Don't look at me!" she cried.

Aly looked at Mom. Mom whispered, "All afternoon."

"Brookester," Aly said, "let me see what Lou did. She's a great haircutter. She styles my hair all the time. Even if Suzy Davis doesn't like my haircut, I do a lot."

"I hate Suzy Davis!" Brooke said, her voice muffled by the blanket.

"I know," Aly said. "But let me see your hair."

Slowly, Brooke pulled the blanket off the top of her head. Her eyes were red from crying. "What do you think?" she sniffled. "Be honest."

Brooke's hair didn't resemble a triangle anymore, which was a very good thing. And there was something that made the waves look almost like curls. So it was actually bouncy more than fluffy. Plus, there were little bits of hair that curled around Brooke's eyes that were actually pretty nice.

"It's cute!" Aly said. "For real, it's cute!"

Brooke peered at Aly as if she didn't quite believe

her. Then, with her reddened eyes, she sent Aly a Secret Sister Eye Message: *Are you telling me the whole truth?*

"It's just not what you're used to," Aly said. "That's all. But it's cute, for real."

Again Brooke sniffled. Then she climbed out of bed and went to look in the mirror that was hanging on the girls' bedroom wall.

And she started crying again.

"I hate it!" she wailed. "It doesn't look like me! Are you sure there's no way to put my braid back on?"

Mom sat down on Brooke's bed. "Brookie, we talked about this. You're still you no matter what your hair looks like. And when you make a decision, you have to take responsibility for it. You told Suzy she could cut your hair. That was your decision. And every decision has consequences."

"I can't go to school like this!" Brooke sobbed. "Please don't make me."

Aly sat next to Mom. She thought about things Brooke liked. She even made a list in her head:

Sparkles

Pink

Yellow

Hair accessories

Animals

Art

"I have an idea!" Aly said. She raced to the girls' closet and took out a basket filled with their hair accessories. She ignored all of the elastics, because Brooke's hair was too short for those now, and instead started pulling out clips, headbands, and sparkly bobby pins.

"You can still use all these fun things in your hair, just like before," Aly explained. "You'll just look like a different version of yourself."

"You think?" Brooke said, picking up a pink glittery headband with a rhinestone cat on one side.

"I know," Aly answered.

Brooke slid on the headband. Aly walked over to her and pulled a couple pieces of hair forward so they curled on Brooke's forehead.

Brooke looked in the mirror again. "Oh!" she said, staring at herself. "Maybe that's not so terrible."

Then she wailed once more. "But I need to wear my glasses to school, and I can't wear my glasses with a headband because it gets too crowded behind my ears!"

Mom started digging through the basket of hair accessories. "Found them!" she said, holding up a set of barrettes made of sparkly, braided rainbow-colored ribbons, with streamers on one side. "Remember when I made these for you a few years ago? I think they'll look great with your glasses."

While Mom clipped the barrettes into Brooke's hair, Aly grabbed Brooke's pink glasses from her drawer. Brooke had a few different pairs, so she could change them to match her outfits. Brooke slipped them on, then looked in the mirror.

"Not terrible at all!" she said, and Aly saw a tiny smile on Brooke's mouth. "I guess I can go to school after all."

Mom breathed a sigh of relief. Now Aly hoped that no one at school would make fun of Brooke's new hair—or even say one word about it. Because she knew that all it would take was one comment for Brooke to hate it all over again.

five

Mellow Yellow

A re you *sure* I look okay?" Brooke asked Aly for probably the thirty-seventh time that morning. "Not just okay, but *better* than okay? People aren't going to think I look like a boy or anything?"

Aly studied her sister. Brooke was wearing a Fairy Teal dress, Mellow Yellow rhinestone sneakers, tons of rainbow-colored necklaces and bracelets, her pink glasses, and the sparkly braided-ribbon barrettes in her hair. "I don't think anyone will mistake you for a boy, Brooke. I promise. And you look great."

Brooke looked in the mirror again. "Maybe I should wear a hat," she said. "Remember the one Grandma got me for my birthday that I didn't like because it wasn't comfortable with my braid? Maybe I should wear that one. Then no one will see my haircut."

Aly pushed her own hair out of her eyes. "I don't think you need it. But how about I find it for you and you bring it to school just in case?"

Brooke went to tug on her braid, but it was gone. Aly saw her sister's lips start to tremble.

"You can tug on your earlobe!" Aly suggested. "Every time you go to tug on your braid, tug on your earlobe instead!" Then she climbed on the step stool to reach the highest shelf in the girls' closet.

"My earlobe?" Brooke said, and then she laughed, giving it a try. "This is actually funny. You do it."

Aly tugged on her earlobe too and then jumped down from the stool with Brooke's hat in her hand.

It was pink with a wide brim and a yellow sunflower on the front. "Here you go," she said, handing it to Brooke.

The girls made their way down the stairs and found Sparkly sitting at the bottom of them.

"Did he come upstairs last night?" Aly asked Brooke. "Did you notice?"

Brooke shook her head. "I was too busy worrying about my hair," she said. "I don't remember."

Aly picked Sparkly up, and he licked her neck. Aly wasn't sure, but she thought he felt a little heavier than usual. Was it possible that he was growing more? The animal shelter had said he was fully grown, but maybe they were wrong.

Aly kissed his head and put him back on the floor. Maybe getting larger took lots of energy and that's why he'd been so quiet lately and hadn't come upstairs last night.

✳ ✳ ✳ ✳ ✳

After breakfast, on the drive to school, instead of chattering nonstop like she usually did, Brooke didn't say a word. Aly knew she was really nervous.

As Mom pulled up to the curb, Aly asked, "Ready, Brookester?"

"I think I need my hat," Brooke whispered. She pulled it on, looked at Aly, and asked, "Okay?" Aly nodded. Then Brooke took a deep breath and opened the car door, with Aly secretly wishing the day was over instead of just begining.

Maybe everything would be okay, though. Because that morning when Aly saw Brooke in the hall once, she'd taken off her hat and she didn't look upset. Aly thought that was a good thing. At least she hoped it was.

At recess Aly was sitting with Lily and Charlotte under the slide. It was one of the prime recess places to sit when you didn't want to be bothered, and Aly, Lily, and Charlotte didn't want to be bothered.

"So . . . do you know if Suzy got into trouble?" Lily asked. "Charlotte said your mom seemed really mad at her yesterday." Lily had gotten to the Sparkle Spa after Suzy and Brooke had left, and she was a little upset that she'd missed the action. So she'd been asking a lot of questions about it.

Aly shrugged. "I don't know. I know my mom called her mom, but really, I mean, it was a dumb, ridiculous idea to cut hair, but it was also kind of dumb of Brooke to volunteer. If no one volunteered, there would have been no haircut. Suzy didn't force her."

"True," said Charlotte, picking up a handful of pebbles and letting them run through her fingers. Then she smiled. "So, what do you think: No haircuts at the Sparkle Spa? Or should we offer Suzy a corner?"

"Ha," Lily said.

Aly smiled too.

"*There* you are!" someone said, bending down under the slide. Aly turned around. That someone was Suzy Davis. "I've been looking all over for you, Aly. Just in case you wanted to say thank you."

"What are you talking about, Suzy?" Charlotte asked, dropping the last of the stones from her hand.

Suzy scooted under the slide, and the girls had to shift to make room for her. "Haven't you heard?" she said. "All anyone is talking about is how cool your sister's haircut is. How it's floppy and fun and how they love her barrettes. So I thought you might want to thank me."

Aly pulled a rock out of the back of her sneaker. "I don't quite think I'm going to thank you, Suzy. Even if it turned out okay in the end, Brooke was really upset yesterday—and this morning, too."

Suzy shrugged. "It's not my fault she didn't realize how great she looked with short hair."

Sometimes Aly couldn't believe how Suzy's brain worked. "Forget it," Aly said. "It's fine." Aly knew Suzy didn't mean to be so . . . Suzy . . . all the time. She just wasn't very good at seeing things from other people's points of view.

"Do you know where she got those barrettes, by the way? Because I'd love some. And I bet Heather would too," Suzy said. Heather was her little sister.

"Oh," Aly said, "my mom made them a while ago."

Suzy's eyes widened. "You should make some more!" she said. "Everyone loves them. Anyway, it's kind of dark and dirty under here. If you decide you want to thank me later, I'll be around."

The moment Suzy had walked out of earshot, Charlotte burst out with, "That girl makes me so annoyed! I can't believe you're friends with her now."

Before Aly could respond, Lily added, "But she has a good idea about those barrettes. Because if people really like them, we could sell them at the Sparkle Spa. And get more money for our donation jar."

Since Mom had said that the girls couldn't charge for their manicure and pedicure services, they'd set up a donation system, collected in a strawberry-shaped teal jar Mom had made in an art school ceramics class. All customers were encouraged to make a donation when they got their nails done, and when the jar was full, the Sparkle Spa staff chose a charity to donate the money to. Since Lily was CFO, she was in charge of the jar and always liked it when they had special Sparkle Spa fund-raisers.

Had Suzy come up with a good idea this time? *Should* they sell barrettes at the Sparkle Spa? Or would that mean less time to polish nails? Aly would have to talk to Brooke.

Six

Back to the Fuchsia

Since it was Monday, the Sparkle Spa wasn't open for business. According to Mom's rules, the girls could open the spa only three days per week—two afternoons on school days and one weekend day. Usually, the girls picked Tuesday, Friday, and Sunday, unless there was a special event. And on the days when the Sparkle Spa was closed, if the girls didn't have an after-school activity, they helped out at their mom's salon, like they used to do before they started their own business.

That Monday, all anyone at True Colors could talk about was Brooke's hair. Luckily, as Suzy had reported, *everyone* at school had loved her short haircut. And when she walked through the salon's front door, the customers went wild. Brooke loved the attention.

"I hadn't realized your hair would curl," Mrs. Franklin said. (Aly hadn't either.)

"It brings attention to your face," Mrs. Howard said. (Aly thought she was right.)

"It's very trendy," Miss Lulu said. (Was that true?)

"And I love those barrettes," Mrs. Bass said.

Mom looked up from manicure station number one when Mrs. Bass said that. "I made those barrettes such a long time ago," she said. "I thought I might want to start a side business, but making them took too much time away from True Colors."

Aly paused. She'd been straightening up the piles

of magazines and collecting polish bottles to return to the polish wall. "Any chance you have leftover supplies?" she asked her mom. "Because a few girls at school asked me about Brooke's barrettes." After recess Annie Wu and Uma had both wanted to know where Brooke had gotten them.

"You know," Mom said, "I think I may have jammed the supplies in the bottom desk drawer in the back room. They'd be in a zipped pouch. Plain barrettes, ribbons, glue—everything I used. You might have to go digging under a lot of paper, though."

Brooke looked over from where she was refilling Carla's little box of nail rhinestones. Carla loved doing manicures with rhinestones for her customers. "Even if there aren't enough supplies to make them for kids at school," Brooke said, "we should make more for me!"

The salon customers laughed, and then Brooke

and Aly raced back into the Sparkle Spa to go hunting in the desk. Sparkly was sitting quietly in his doggie bed.

"Where are they?" Brooke said, opening a desk drawer. Then she stopped. "Oh," she said. "Oh."

Aly walked over. "Your braid," she said. "I'm sorry you saw it. I couldn't bring myself to throw it out."

Brooke sat down on the floor. "My new haircut turned out okay, but I'd be sad throwing out my braid too. Maybe there's something else we could do with it."

"Let's make a list of ideas," Aly offered. She pulled out a piece of paper:

Things to Do with Brooke's Braid
- Hang it on the bedroom wall
- Wrap it in tissue paper and put it in the closet

- Make it into a doll
- Stuff it in a pillow
- Throw it away

"I don't know about any of these," Aly said, looking back over the list.

"How about . . . make it into a wig?" Brooke said.

Aly looked at her sister. "Wait!" she said. "Remember when Mrs. Rosenberg, the secretary at school, was sick last year and she wore that wig that was practically the color of Back to the Fuchsia?"

Brooke nodded.

"Well," Aly said, "I wonder if there are people who are sick who might want to use your hair to make a wig."

Brooke was nodding so hard now that her short hair was flopping all over the place. It made Aly smile.

"Yes!" Brooke agreed. "That's exactly what we

should do with my hair. But . . . how do we find people who might need it?"

"I'll look it up online. And we can ask Mom or Joan," Aly said. "In the meantime, let's put your braid back in the drawer and see about this barrette business."

After a bit of rummaging around in the desk, Aly and Brooke found the zippered pouch with all the barrette materials in it. There were thirty barrettes, so knowing Mom, Aly figured that meant there would be enough ribbon to make all thirty of them. Brooke took one out of her hair so the girls could see exactly what their mom had done.

"Look," Brooke said. "She braided four pieces of ribbon together, tied a knot, then left a few inches for the streamers. Then she tied a tiny knot at the end of each streamer."

Aly took the barrette from her sister. "And it

seems like she glued the braided part to the barrette, then tucked the top of the braid under so you can't see the fraying ribbon at the top edge. We can make these no problem."

In fact, with Aly braiding and Brooke gluing and knotting, they made twelve barrettes in an hour.

When it was time to clean up, Brooke asked, "Should we set these up near the donation jar so our customers can buy them?"

But Aly was only half listening. She was still thinking about Mrs. Rosenberg.

Brooke repeated the question.

"I'm not sure, Brooke," she finally answered. "I might have another plan."

Brooke zipped up the remaining ribbons in the pouch. "Okay. Tell me when you're ready."

But somehow, thinking about Mrs. Rosenberg also made Aly think about Sparkly. Could he be sick?

Is that why he seemed so quiet and tired and heavier than usual? Aly swallowed that thought down.

Before bed that night, Aly found just what she was looking for: a charity called Loving Locks, which donated wigs to people who had lost their hair because they were sick. The charity needed hair that was at least ten inches long, and Aly knew Brooke's hair was much longer than that. Plus, they took donations in money as well as in hair.

Aly was ready to share her idea with her sister, but Brooke had already fallen asleep. She was tempted to wake her up to tell her about her plan, but she didn't want to jinx it. Tomorrow, then, she decided—first thing.

Seven
Red Rover

The next morning, over cereal and bananas, Aly presented her plan to Brooke. She even cleared her throat first, to make her announcement more official.

"I think," Aly began, "we should donate your hair to Loving Locks. It's a charity I found online that can turn it into a wig for someone who's sick. And we should donate the money from all the barrettes we sell to that charity too." She slid the piece of paper she'd printed out last night across the table to Brooke.

Brooke read the rules. "My hair is longer than ten inches, right?" she asked.

Aly nodded.

"And I never dyed it any colors, and it's stored in a braid, and it's not in dreadlocks."

Aly nodded again.

"And if we make enough money from the barrettes, then maybe we'll be able to pay for the cost of turning my hair into a wig!"

"That's exactly what I was thinking," Aly told her sister.

"Wait!" Brooke said, stabbing the air with her spoon. "Let's include the money from our donation jar too."

Aly smiled. "Perfect idea, Brookester," she said.

As Aly took another spoonful of cereal, she heard Sparkly whine. She looked over at him and saw that he hadn't eaten much of his breakfast. Now she was really starting to get worried. She had no choice—she'd have to tell Mom.

That day, Brooke wore two of the barrettes she and Aly had made the day before. At least fifteen girls at school asked where they could get them. Even better, the same fifteen girls said they never knew short hair could be so cool until they saw Brooke with her barrettes. Even Caleb complimented Brooke's haircut—and her barrettes.

Whenever people asked, the Tanner girls said that starting this weekend, the barrettes would be available at the Sparkle Spa for $2.00 each and that the money would go to a good cause.

But even more surprising was what happened at the end of the day. While Aly was waiting for Brooke on the steps of the school, Violet Quinn, a second grader, ran up to her, and she had a haircut just like Brooke's.

"What do you think of my new hair, Aly?" Violet asked, spinning around so Aly could check her out from all sides.

"It looks awesome," Aly said. Violet and her sister, Daisy, were both Sparkle Spa customers.

"Yesterday I was getting my hair trimmed. Lou was talking about the cute cut she had just given another customer. She thought it would look good on me, and it turned out that the customer was Brooke Tanner. I said I wanted her haircut too!"

Violet turned around again, to show off her hair. "Brooke's haircut is so, so cool. When I got home, Daisy was jealous. I think she's going to get her hair cut the same way today."

"Really?" Aly asked, tugging her backpack straps.

Violet nodded. Daisy had pretty long hair. Come to think of it, Violet had too.

All of a sudden, Aly had a terrific idea. One that

would mean a side trip on the way to the salon after school.

"I'm going to come to the Sparkle Spa this weekend for those cool barrettes Brooke has," Violet told her. "If Daisy winds up with a new style, I'll buy some for her too."

Aly smiled at Violet. "Well, we'll be there," she said. "Don't forget to let me or Charlotte know if you want a manicure or pedicure appointment this weekend."

"I'll ask my mom," Violet said. "I've been thinking nail polish would go really well with my new haircut."

Aly laughed. "I think nail polish goes really well with *all* haircuts."

Violet laughed too and skipped over to her mom's car in the pickup circle in front of school.

When Brooke came out of the building with Sophie following her, Aly told them, "We have to make a detour today on the way to the Sparkle Spa. Did you see Violet's new haircut?"

Brooke grinned from ear to ear. "Just like mine."

"Exactly," Aly answered as the girls started walking. "And Daisy might be getting one today. Her hair's almost as long as yours used to be. We absolutely have to tell Lou about Loving Locks."

"Maybe I should get my hair cut," Sophie said as the group walked into Skip to My Lou. Her dark, straight hair came to about the bottom of her shoulder blades. "How many inches do you think it is?"

"We need something to measure it with," Brooke said. She asked Mallory, the salon receptionist, if she had a ruler. Fortunately, Mallory found a plastic one that looked like it had at one point lived in someone's school desk.

"Measure it from the tip-top of my head," Sophie requested.

Brooke started at Sophie's part, gently pulling a strand away from her head to check its length. "There's the first twelve inches," she said, marking the spot on Sophie's hair with her finger where the ruler ended, then moving the ruler down. "And another six inches. So you measure eighteen inches," she reported.

"How many inches do I need in order to donate?" she asked.

"Ten," Aly and Brooke answered together.

"Can you measure eight inches of my hair?" Sophie asked. "From the top again."

Eight inches got Sophie's hair to her chin. If she did cut it, it would wind up quite a bit longer than Brooke's hair.

Aly spied a hair magazine nearby and skimmed through it until she found a model with a chin-length bob. "Look!" she said, showing the magazine to Sophie. "If you cut ten inches, you hair could look like this girl's. That is, if you have the same type of hair as hers."

Brooke sighed. "That, apparently, is a very important part of haircuts. A part Suzy Davis was clueless about."

Sophie and Aly giggled. Sophie carefully studied the magazine. "I'll do it," she said. "And I want to donate my hair like Brooke is."

Just as she said that, Lou walked over. "What can I do to help you girls?" she asked. "Mallory said you needed to see me."

Aly started, "We want to—" But Brooke cut her off.

"Remember a few days ago when you gave me a haircut?" she asked.

Lou nodded. "Of course I do."

"Well, Aly saved my braid. And we're going to donate it to a charity called Loving Locks, which makes wigs for sick people who need them. We were thinking that maybe whenever anyone with long hair gets their hair cut here, they might like to donate their hair too. And since this is your salon, maybe you could be the one to ask them?"

Brooke stopped for air and then continued. "Because Aly knows that Daisy Quinn has an appointment to get her hair cut to match Violet's. So if you could tell your customers about Loving Locks and the wigs and the donations, that would be really nice."

Aly smiled. She couldn't have said it better herself. But she did hand the information sheet on Loving Locks to Lou. "This is what it says on their website," she said.

"You know," Lou said, "this is wonderful idea. I can't believe I never thought of it myself before. Why waste all that hair when it could help someone in need? I'll make copies of this and make sure Mallory distributes it around the salon, particularly to anyone with long hair who comes in for a haircut."

"And, Lou," Sophie piped up, "will you cut my hair to my chin, so I can donate my hair too?"

"Of course I can, Sophie," Lou answered. "But not today. You need a parent to call for an appointment."

The girls said their good-byes and headed to the Sparkle Spa. The spa wasn't going to be open that day—they'd pushed their work day to Wednesday this week at the request of the Auden Angels soccer team—but the girls wanted to finish making the barrettes.

"You know," Sophie said as she braided some of the sparkly ribbons, "if we're starting to sell these on Saturday, maybe we could offer a special manicure to go along with it. We could charge a certain amount and donate that money to Loving Locks too."

"Well, we'd already planned to give the donation jar money to Loving Locks," Brooke said, blowing on the barrette she was making to help dry the glue.

"Yeah, but I know what Sophie means," Aly said. "For regular Sparkle Spa services, people donate any amount they want. But if we created one of our special occasion manicures in honor of Loving Locks, we could set a five-dollar contribution. Then we'd have even more money to donate."

Brooke nodded. "Got it," she said. "And I know the perfect manicure." She chose two polish colors—Red Rover and Yellow Submarine—and took Aly's hand in hers. She painted Aly's thumb bright red, and when it dried, she painted a neat yellow stripe right across the top. "It's like a colorful French manicure," she said, "so it'll be easy for us to do. But at the same time it looks special."

Aly inspected her thumb. It looked pretty cool.

"And we can do whatever colors anyone wants," Brooke added. "Not just these."

Aly knew that Charlotte and Lily would love the idea too. Charlotte loved all special events at the Sparkle Spa, and Lily loved all chances to make— and donate—more money.

"Isn't it amazing how my haircut is turning into a way to help so many other people?" Brooke said.

Aly realized she was right. Only Brooke could turn a Suzy Davis disaster into something wonderful.

eight
Right as Rain

That night, once again, Sparkly didn't eat much of his dinner. Aly couldn't wait another second. She had to tell Brooke and her mom.

Brooke looked like she might cry. "I don't want Sparkly to be sick!" she said.

Mom hugged her. "Me neither, Brookie," she said. "And chances are he's not. But let's take him to the vet to get checked out."

It made Aly feel so much better that Mom was in charge now. But she wouldn't feel completely better until she knew what was wrong with Sparkly.

✳ ✳ ✳ ✳ ✳

Because the entire Auden Elementary girls' soccer team was booked for rainbow sparkle pedicures on Wednesday, Aly knew there wasn't going to be an inch to move or a moment to spare at the Sparkle Spa that afternoon. A few of the players had asked for manicures too, not just Anjuli, the goalie who *always* got a manicure.

As the Tanner girls racewalked to True Colors after school with Sophie, Charlotte, and Lily, Brooke asked Aly, "Do you think Mom made a doctor's appointment for Sparkly yet? I've been thinking about him all day."

"Me too," Aly said. "But I'm not sure. Sometimes animal doctors are like people doctors. Unless it's an emergency, it can be hard to get a last-minute appointment."

"I've been thinking about Sparkly too," said Lily. "Maybe he just has a cold."

Aly had filled her friends in on the Sparkly situation at lunch. Aly hoped that's all it was.

When they reached the salon, Brooke and Aly hurried over to their mom, who was sitting at the reception desk. "How's Sparkly?" they both asked at the same time.

Mom smiled. "Well," she said, "we didn't need to go to the vet. Sparkly's fine."

"But—" Aly started to say.

"Carla, would you like to explain it to the girls, or should I?" Mom asked. Carla had just finished up a manicure for Mr. Andrews at manicure station three. He always like to have his nails polished with Right as Rain, which was clear with extra shine. Carla walked over to the reception desk.

"I'm so sorry, girls," she said. "I was trying to be nice to Sparkly, but apparently, two dog cookies a day is too many for a dog that tiny."

"You were giving him *two* dog cookies a day?" Brooke asked. "When? How come? Where did you get them?"

Carla ran her fingers through her bangs. "Delish Doggie Treats were on sale. I thought he might like to eat them while he waited for you girls in his corner during the school day. And he *loved* them, so I started giving him a couple every day. When your mom mentioned needing to take time off to bring Sparkly to the vet, I told her about the cookies," she said, leaning against the counter.

"We called the vet, and he's sure that's why Sparkly's been acting so strange," Mom added.

"So no more cookies," Carla said. "I promise. And I'm so sorry I made you worry—and made Sparkly feel ill."

Aly knew that the manicurists played with Sparkly while she and Brooke were at school, but she had no idea they were feeding him too.

"It's okay," Aly said. "We're just relieved he's not really sick."

Brooke started to say something, but she instead headed back to the Sparkle Spa. The rest of the girls followed.

"Well, that turned out well," Lily said. "No cold or anything."

Brooke plopped down on the floor to do her homework. "All I'm going to say," she said, "is that a person shouldn't give another person's dog a cookie without permission."

Aly laughed. "I agree," she said. She pulled Sparkly into her lap, scratched him behind his ears, and worked on her homework as quickly as she could while he licked the crease of her elbow.

Now that she knew Sparkly was fine, she could focus on getting through the rush today at the

Sparkle Spa and then look forward to Saturday's fund-raiser. Of all the different Sparkle Spa events, Aly felt sure that this one for Loving Locks was just about the most important. It *had* to be a success.

nine

Purple You May Know

Aly didn't sleep well Friday night. She tossed and turned for over an hour, flipping her pillow over and over to find a cool spot, counting hundreds of kittens and puppies, worrying about making enough money for Loving Locks, and wondering if she could function on barely any sleep.

She and Brooke arrived at the Sparkle Spa super early on Saturday, and Charlotte walked in two minutes later. She'd made really cute and colorful signs about the prices of the special occasion manicure and the barrettes, and she set to work taping them around the salon.

"Are we limiting the barrette purchasing?" she asked.

"What do you mean?" Brooke said. She was creating a pretty display for the barrettes on a pillowcase the color of Purple You May Know.

"Well," Charlotte said, "we only have twenty-eight barrettes to sell, meaning fourteen pairs. So only fourteen people can buy a set of barrettes. And practically *everyone* at school said they want to buy them. So should we limit them to only one per person?"

Aly was straightening up the polish wall. "But what if it was all talk?" she said. "What if only four people want to actually buy them?"

Charlotte scratched her head. "Well," she suggested, "how about we say one pair per person at first? And if we start selling a lot them, we can always limit it to one barrette per person later."

Aly sent Brooke a Secret Sister Eye Message: *Okay?* Brooke sent her answer right back: *Okay.*

"Sounds good to me," Aly told Charlotte.

The Sparkle Spa was supposed to open at 10:00 a.m., but by 9:30, Daisy, Violet, Maxie, Joelle, Uma, Annie, and Clementine were already waiting in line outside the door to buy barrettes.

"That's almost half our entire inventory," Brooke whispered to Aly.

Aly counted the number of girls. "Actually, if we sell the barrettes in pairs, that's exactly half," she said. "I think we may need to start a waiting list and then buy materials to make more this week."

Charlotte held up her clipboard. "I was thinking the same thing," she said, showing them a piece of paper with numbers written down the side. "I was just going to show you the form I'm making."

"Great minds think alike," Brooke told her. "And ours are super great."

A few minutes later Sophie and Lily showed up. Lily planted herself near the donations table, and Sophie took her spot at her manicure station.

At exactly 10:00, according to Aly's purple polka-dot watch, they opened for business.

First, the Sparkle Spa team started selling barrettes. There were nine people in line by then who all wanted a pair, so eighteen of the twenty-eight barrettes were gone within ten minutes.

Next, the manicures started.

And then they ran out of barrettes.

"What do you mean there aren't any left?" Eliza Perez asked when she walked into the salon an hour after they opened. Her dark wavy hair hung down to her waist.

"You can be the first person on our waiting list," Charlotte said. "You'll get the first set of barrettes as soon as Aly and Brooke make more."

Eliza didn't seem thrilled, but then she said, "Actually, that should be fine, because I'm not getting my hair cut until next week."

Brooke couldn't be happier. "You're cutting your hair too?"

Eliza nodded. "Just like yours," she said. "So I can donate my hair to Loving Locks and then wear those cool barrettes."

"I decided I'm going to cut mine like Sophie's," Annie said.

Brooke looked at Aly like she couldn't believe it. "Wow," she said. "I never thought that letting Suzy cut my hair would get so many other people to cut theirs too!"

The rest of the day went off without a hitch. At five o'clock the girls flopped on the couch and pillows in the waiting area as Lily counted their money. "Fifty-six dollars from barrettes," she said, "and between regular manicures and our special of the day, two hundred seventy-three dollars and seventeen cents. Uma even gave us the extra change in her pocket. Our grand total is three hundred and twenty-nine dollars and seventeen cents!"

"Whoa!" Brooke said.

"Yes!" Charlotte cheered.

Aly smiled. "That's really awesome, guys."

As they started cleaning up, Mrs. Rosenberg poked her head in.

"Hi, girls," she said. "I was having my nails done at your mom's salon, and she told me what you were all doing today. You have no idea what your donation will mean to people. I'm going to add one hundred dollars to however much you raised today."

Lily gasped.

"Thank you!" Aly said.

"Yes, thank you!" Brooke and Sophie and Charlotte echoed.

"No, thank *you*," Mrs. Rosenberg said. "There are lots of things that are pretty awful about being sick, and one of them is how . . . well . . . *non*sparkly you feel. Having a beautiful wig really does help sometimes."

Mrs. Rosenberg gave each girl a hug, then left.

"Do you think everyone feels that way?" Brooke asked. "Because that makes me think we should offer manicures at the hospital."

"That, Brooke Tanner," Aly said, "is a very interesting and inspiring idea." Aly decided she'd look into it. It really was true that feeling sparkly on the outside sometimes made people feel sparkly on the inside— and the opposite was true as well. Aly had learned that just last week when Brooke didn't like her haircut.

It was amazing, Aly thought to herself, how much good a little sparkle could do.

ten

Blue Suede Shoes

I love this new ribbon," Brooke said. "It's the same color as Sunvisor. It goes so nicely with the bright red and orange we bought last week."

It was a Saturday morning a few weeks later, and Aly and Brooke were sitting together in their living room making barrettes. Sparkly was jumping around and barking, like he was offering advice on which colors to use.

Since the barrettes were such a hit, the girls kept making them—and kept donating all the proceeds to Loving Locks.

Mid-braid, Aly heard a car pull into the driveway. Sparkly went crazy, racing for the front door.

"Dad?" Brooke asked.

Aly grinned.

The girls went racing for the front door too.

Dad walked in smelling like an airplane, with his briefcase strap slung over his shoulder, his suitcase rolling behind him, and a stack of letters in one hand. "Did you ladies forget to get the mail?" he asked.

Mom had come up next to the girls. "Oops," she said, and leaned over to give Dad a kiss.

"Sorry, Dad," Aly said, taking the mail from him. Even though all the Tanner women were CEOs, going to the mailbox while Dad was gone was not their best skill.

Aly scanned through all the envelopes, pulling out one addressed to Brooke. "Brookester, you've got mail," she said, handing over the letter.

Aly quickly sifted through the rest of the mail. Nothing for her. There rarely was. Or for Brooke, either, for that matter. So this letter must be something special.

Brooke tore it open. A photograph fell to the floor. She bent to pick it up, then unfolded the note that came with it. "Whoa," she said. "I can't believe it. Whoa."

Brooke was rarely speechless.

"What is it?" Aly asked her sister.

Brooke handed the note and the photograph to Aly.

Dear Brooke,

Thank you so much for donating your hair to Loving Locks so that a wig could be made for me. Your hair is just like mine—the same color and everything. I wanted to show you how it looks and how happy your kindness—and hair—has made me. I felt so much better when I put it on.

XOXO,

Arianna

Aly looked at the picture. It was of a girl who looked maybe nine or ten years old. She had Blue Suede Shoes–colored eyes and a huge smile on her face.

"You know what I think?" Brooke said. "I think I'm going to grow my hair long again just so I can cut it off and help someone else."

Aly fingered her own hair. "Me too," she said.

Mom read the letter, then leaned over and hugged both girls. "It's one thing to be smart, it's another thing to be strong, and yet another to be sparkly," she said. "But you girls are kind and caring and compassionate too."

"We got some good ones," Dad said. "Right?"

"We sure did," Mom answered.

Mom's and Dad's smiles looked as big as Arianna's did in her picture. Aly decided she wanted to be the kind of person—for her whole life—who did everything she could to make people smile just like that.

How to Give Yourself (or a Friend!) a Loving Locks Special Occasion Pedicure

By Aly (and Brooke!)

* .. * .. * .. * .. * .. *

What you need:

Paper towels

Polish remover

Cotton balls

(Or you can just use more paper towels.)

Clear polish

Two different color polishes

(You can choose any colors you want, but we like red and yellow best for this one.)

What you do:

1. Place some paper towels on the floor—or wherever you're going to put your feet—so you don't have to worry about drips or spills. (We spend so much time worrying about drips and spills! Luckily, in the Sparkle Spa we have the kind of floor that is easy to clean, but there are a lot of floors that aren't!)

2. Take a cotton ball or a folded-up paper towel and put some polish remover on it. If you have polish on your toes already, use enough to take it off. If you don't, just rub the remover over your nails once to remove any dirt. (Because dirt can make your polish look clumpy, and also because you shouldn't have dirty feet anyway!) Nail polish sticks better when you do this

before polishing. (If you can figure out why, let us know.)

3. Rip off two more paper towels. Roll the first one into a tube and twist it so it stays that way. Then weave it back and forth between your toes to separate them a little bit. After that, do the same thing with the second paper towel on your other foot. You might need to tuck it in around your pinky toe if it pops up and gets in your way while you polish—you can also cut the towel to make it shorter. (Aly doesn't like ripping it because sometimes too much gets ripped and then you have to start over with a brand-new paper towel.)

4. Open your clear polish and apply a coat to each nail. Then close the clear bottle up tight. (You

can go in any order, but Aly usually starts with the big toes and works her way to the pinkies. I do too.)

5. Open the first colored polish. Use it to polish all your toes. Put the cap back on tight. (The tightness is important, in case someone—or something, like your dog—knocks over your polish.)

6. Repeat step five.

7. Open the second colored polish. Wipe the polish brush against the side of the bottle so there's no excess to drip off. Then swipe the brush very, very carefully straight across the top of your big toes. (You might get some on your skin. Don't worry about that. Just wait until the polish dries and wipe it off, either with nail

polish remover or with soap and water the next time you take a bath or shower.) If the color of the stripe doesn't look as bright as you want it, blow on your big toes a little to dry them, then do the same thing all over again, adding another swipe of color on top of the first. Screw the cap back on the polish bottle tightly.

8. Blow on all your toes or just let them dry for a few minutes. Then apply a clear top coat. Close the bottle up tight. (Really tight!)

9. Now your toes have to fully dry. You can fan them for a long time, or you can sit and make a bracelet or read a book or watch TV or talk to a friend (or your sister!) until they're dry. You can also call around or use the computer to search for things you can do to help out in your community

and read about them while you're waiting. It usually takes about twenty minutes for toes to dry, but it could take longer. (That's why we try to find fun things to do while our nails dry. Otherwise, sitting in one place for twenty minutes is bor-ing.)

Now you have your very own beautiful Loving Locks special occasion pedicure! Even after your polish is dry, you probably shouldn't wear socks and sneaker-type shoes for a while. Bare feet or sandals are better so all your hard work doesn't get smudged. (And so you can show off your striped big toes!)

Happy polishing!

✳ ⋅⋆⋅ ✳ ⋅⋆⋅ ✳ ⋅⋆⋅ ✳ ⋅⋆⋅ ✳ ⋅⋆⋅ ✳